Andi Under the Big Top

Circle C Stepping Stones

Circle C Stepping Stones #2

Andi Under the Big Top

Susan K. Marlow

Kregel
Publications

Printed in the United States of America
17 18 19 20 21 22 23 24 25 26 / 5 4 3 2 1

Contents

New Words

acrobat—a person who performs skillful gymnastic acts like tumbling and tightrope walking

big top—the large tent where the circus performances take place

calliope—(kuh-LIE-uh-pee) a musical instrument that produces sounds by pushing steam through large pipes of differing lengths

gelding—a male horse that cannot father a foal

green broke—describes a horse that knows the basics and has carried a rider but is not completely trained

jack-in-the-box—a toy box containing a figure (like a clown) on a spring that pops up when the lid is opened by turning a crank

menagerie—a collection of wild or unusual animals on display

paddock—a small fenced pasture where horses are kept or exercised

ringmaster—the person who announces the performances in the circus ring

sideshow—a small show at a circus or fair that often displays odd twists of nature like a two-headed calf

stilts—upright poles with supports for the feet that allow a person to walk high above the ground

surrey—a horse-drawn carriage with two wide bench seats and a canopy top

trapeze—a very high swing that circus performers use for doing tricks

Uncle Sam—a symbol of the United States, pictured as a man dressed in red, white, and blue

⇥ CHAPTER 1 ⇤

Here Comes the Circus

Late Summer 1877

Andi Carter stood next to the hitching post and scratched at her hot, sticky black stockings. There wasn't a speck of shade in the entire churchyard. A straw hat kept the sun out of Andi's eyes, but it couldn't keep away the scorching heat.

"I know you're hot too," she told the matched pair of bay horses hitched to her family's surrey.

Jingo and Barney stood drooping, heads down. Their black tails flicked at the buzzing flies. Their reddish-brown bodies quivered. Biting insects gave them no peace.

Andi felt squirmy too, but it wasn't because of any

pesky flies. "Why do grown-ups have to stand around so long after church and talk, talk, talk?" she asked.

Neither horse gave so much as a nicker in reply.

Andi scratched harder and looked across the yard.

Mother was chatting with Mrs. King by the church steps. Big brothers Justin, Chad, and Mitch had found a group of ranchers. Even Melinda, who usually wanted to go home as fast as Andi did, giggled with two other girls her age.

Moisture dripped down the back of Andi's neck. She rubbed away the prickly feeling.

"Hey, Andi!"

Cory Blake skidded to a stop next to the horses. Dust puffed up around his high-top shoes. His Sunday go-to-meeting clothes were rumpled and dark with sweat.

The dust tickled Andi's nose. She sneezed. "You're crazy to run around in this heat."

Cory adjusted his cap farther down over his straw-colored hair. "Can't be helped. I've been looking for you." He grabbed her hand. "C'mon. I wanna show you something."

Andi didn't budge. "I better not. We're leaving in a minute or two." She let out an impatient breath. "I hope."

Cory laughed. "I bet you're not." His blue-gray eyes told Andi he knew something she didn't.

Andi slid her hand from Cory's sweaty grip and

glanced back toward the church steps. Another lady had joined Mother.

"Oh no." Andi groaned. Gossipy Mrs. Evans never stopped talking.

"Your ma won't be getting away from her for at least another fifteen minutes," Cory said. "Plenty of time to show you." He pointed to the Fresno Hotel just across the street. "It's not far."

"All right." Andi patted Barney's nose. "I'll be back."

Cory shouted a happy *yee-haw* and took off.

When Andi caught up with her friend, he was studying the south side of the two-story hotel. "Looky here." He grinned. "Have you ever seen such a sight?"

Andi's eyes went straight to the three large posters pasted on the building. She caught her breath. "Oh my!"

Cory was right.

Never in all her nine years had Andi seen such bright colors or more alive-looking paintings. A lion with a wide-open mouth stood on his hind legs. He looked ready to gobble somebody up in one bite. The brave lion tamer, dressed in his African safari clothes, held only a whip.

"'Clyde Bates in single-handed battle with the most savage jungle beasts known to man,'" Andi read in a whisper.

"Circus posters went up all over town yesterday," Cory said. "Pa let the men paste two of them on our livery stable." He smiled wider. "I helped smooth out the wrinkles and air bubbles."

"The circus?" Andi's heart skipped a beat. "Coming to Fresno? When? Where will they set up the tents? How long will it—"

"The posters tell you everything," Cory said. "Me and Jack read 'em all when we followed the men around. We saw posters with bareback riders and trapeze artists. A man juggling burning torches. Tigers and tightrope walkers and"—he took a deep breath and recited—"'the most daring feats of skill and courage ever seen on this American continent.'"

Andi stepped closer to the posters. Her heart beat fast. In sparkly reds, blues, and yellows, Miss Minnie Mae, the champion female bareback rider of the world, stood atop two matching palominos. The horses leaped through a ring of blazing fire.

Another poster showing acrobats and a clown read: FREE STREET PARADE SATURDAY MORNING. Just below the lettering, Andi read the performance times: THREE O'CLOCK AND SEVEN O'CLOCK AUGUST 25TH. **ONE DAY ONLY!**

Cory placed his hand over the lion's head. "This is the best circus act. A roaring lion. The crack of the lion tamer's whip, the—"

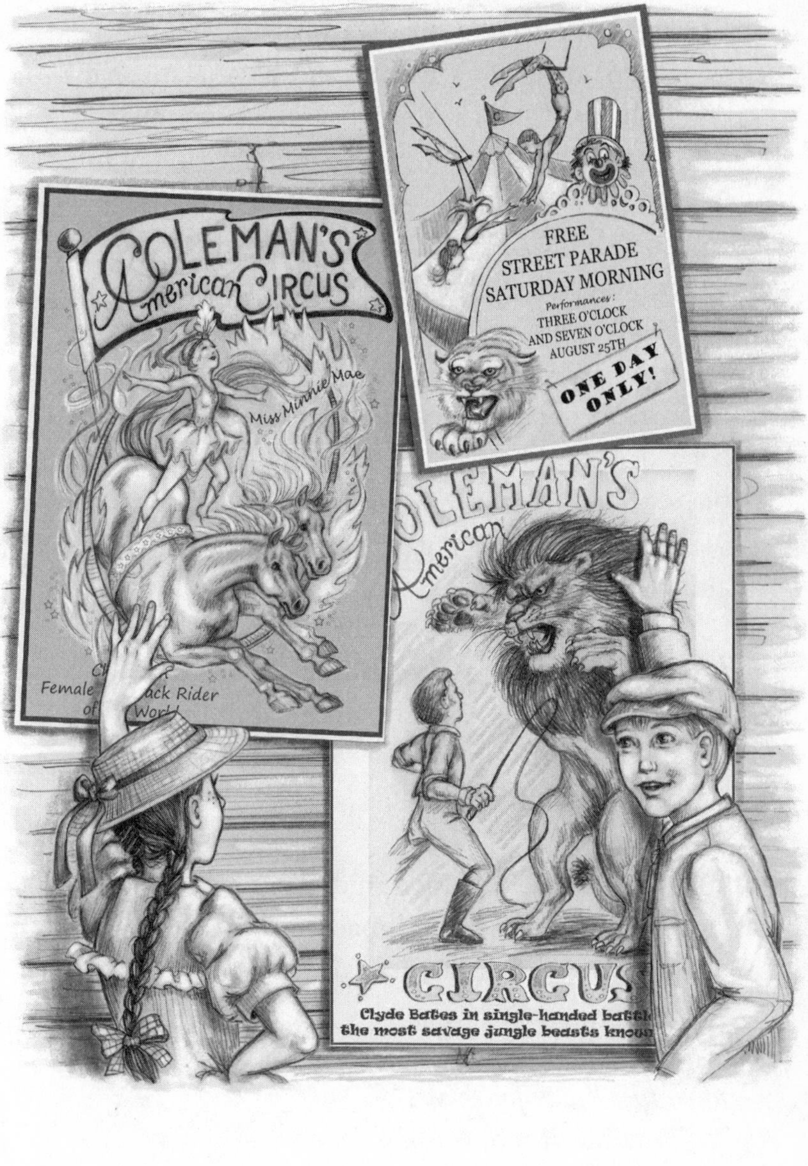
COLEMAN'S
American CIRCUS
Miss Minnie Mae
FREE
STREET PARADE
SATURDAY MORNING
Performances :
THREE O'CLOCK
AND SEVEN O'CLOCK
AUGUST 25TH
ONE DAY ONLY!
OLEMAN'S
American
CIRCUS
Clyde Bates in single-handed
the most savage jungle beasts

"How would you know?" Andi interrupted. "You've never been to the circus."

The painted lion's mouth and huge teeth made Andi shiver. Cory was mighty brave to touch it. *Show-off!* She slapped her hand over the ring of fire. "*This* is the best act."

Cory huffed. "You've never been to the circus either. Maybe it isn't real fire at all."

"And maybe it's not a real lion," Andi said. "Maybe—"

"I've been to the circus," Melinda said from behind Andi. She strolled up to the posters. In her big-sister way she waved her hand to take them all in. "It's all real. The jugglers, the acrobats, the wild animals. Everything."

Cory's hand slid down the poster. He stared at Melinda, eyes wide and admiring.

No fair! Andi thought. Why did the youngest child in the family always miss the excitement? "When did you see a circus?" *I probably wasn't even born yet.*

"I was nine," Melinda said. "It wasn't a big circus like this one. The railroad track had just been put down. A small circus train came through the valley."

Andi's face puckered into a scowl. *If Melinda was nine, then I was four years—*

"You saw it too, Andi."

14

"I did?" Her eyebrows shot up.

Melinda nodded. "You sat on Father's lap and spilled lemonade down your dress. All over Father too." She started laughing. "He jumped a foot in surprise."

Sweat suddenly beaded Andi's forehead, and not because of the noonday heat. Melinda's words had jogged a long-forgotten memory. "I was scared," she whispered.

"That's right."

"What was I scared of?" Andi glanced at the poster-lion's gaping mouth. "The lions?" That fear was not hard to imagine. "Or maybe the elephants?"

"Not at all," Melinda said, smiling. "There weren't any elephants or lions. Just a few acrobats, some jugglers, and a bareback rider. And clowns. You were terrified of the clowns. One came up and tried to shake your hand. You shrieked and lost your lemonade."

"You're scared of *clowns*, Andi?" Cory laughed so hard he held his stomach. Then he wiped his eyes and pointed to the top poster. "You're scared of that smiling, silly-looking clown?"

Andi had no memory of the clowns. "Course not. Melinda's making up a story."

"Am not. Ask Mother or the boys." Melinda lost her smile. "But there was one truly frightening part of that circus."

"What?" Cory asked. "Did an acrobat fall off the high wire?"

"No. It was Mitch. He was fourteen, just my age. All he talked about was running off to join the circus."

"Like being a part of it?" Cory's eyes gleamed.

Melinda nodded. "He went on and on about the colors, the excitement, no school." She bit her lip. "I was scared I'd wake up one morning and find Mitch gone."

Andi caught her breath. "Gone for keeps?"

"Yes."

Andi could not imagine life without her cheerful, laughing big brother. When Chad bossed her too much, she often ran to Mitch. He always took her side.

"Father didn't let Mitch out of his sight until the circus left town," Melinda said. "He also kept a close eye on him for a whole week afterward."

She paused and glanced at the posters. Then she held out her hand. "Come on, Andi. Mother sent me to find you. It's time to go home."

Andi took her sister's hand, but her gaze stayed fixed on the poster of the bareback rider. Glittery costume, happy smile.

No school. A thrill shot through Andi.

She understood Mitch's feelings exactly.

⚜ CHAPTER 2 ⚜

Ready, Set, Go

Andi counted the days until the Saturday street parade. Her head was crammed full of circus plans. Not once all week did she ask anyone to saddle Taffy.

I am a world-champion bareback rider on my prancing golden steed.

Andi and Taffy jumped logs and small fences. With her eyes closed, she imagined the two of them leaping through the circus poster's flaming ring. *Just like Miss Minnie Mae!*

Later that week, when she swung from the rope swing in her favorite tree, Andi pretended to be a trapeze artist. She hung upside down and let the blood rush to her head.

Then her fingers slipped.

Thud! Andi hit the ground. She landed flat on her back and got the breath knocked out of her.

A grinning ranch hand walked by just then. He picked her up and brushed her off. "You hurt, Miss Andi?"

It took a few seconds to get enough breath to speak. "No. I don't think so. But I don't think I want to be a trapeze artist anymore." She looked around the yard. Her gaze fell on Duke, Prince, and King, the ranch dogs.

A lion tamer!

Andi cheered right up. She yanked the buggy whip from its socket and lined up the dogs in a straight row. "I'm in single-handed battle with you savage jungle beasts!"

Crack! She snapped the whip above their heads.

Yipping, the dogs scattered and ducked behind the barn.

"Come back here, you lions!" Andi hollered.

"Enough nonsense, madame lion tamer." Chad took the whip away. "This belongs in the buggy, not left lying on the ground for me to pick up later."

Andi tried to snatch the whip, but her brother was too tall. "Give it back!"

Chad shook his head. "Nope. You never put anything away." He shooed her off to play someplace else.

Andi scuffed the dirt. *I guess it's back to bareback riding.*

⚜ ⚜

On Saturday morning, Andi was up before the rooster stopped crowing. She finished her barn chores and slid into her breakfast chair with a sunny smile.

"May we go to the street parade, Mother? It's free. The circus posters said so."

Mother sighed. "I have too much to do this morning, sweetheart. Besides, I'd rather not stand around wilting under the sun for two hours." She shook her head. "No, I think this afternoon's show will be enough excitement for one day."

Andi slumped. *I'm not a flower. I won't wilt.*

She didn't speak her thoughts out loud, though. Mother usually put her foot down even harder when Andi argued or talked back.

She peeked at Melinda. *Your turn.*

"I heard the entire town is turning out for it," Melinda said. "The weather has cooled a few degrees. We don't have to stay for the whole parade. Please, Mother?"

Mother hesitated.

"How about this?" Mitch asked. He swallowed his last drops of coffee. "I'll take the girls to the parade. After all, how often does the circus come to town?"

Joy bubbled up inside Andi when Mother said yes. "Yippee!" She shot out of her chair and threw her arms around Mitch's neck. "Thank you!"

"Don't keep them out too long," Mother said. "And, Andrea?"

"Yes, Mother. I know. I'll wear my hat and—"

"Change out of those overalls and into something decent for visiting town."

Andi didn't argue.

She was dressed and waiting in the barn when her brother and sister walked in. "Please, Mitch. No buggy. Can we ride? I need to make up for all those weeks when my arm was healing."

She held it up. "See? Good as new. Doesn't hurt a bit."

"Sure." Mitch turned to Melinda. "If it's all right with you, Sis."

Melinda eyed her horse. "So long as you saddle Panda for me."

"Don't saddle Taffy," Andi piped up. "I'm a champion bareback rider."

Mitch gave her a puzzled look.

"I'm a *sitting-down* bareback rider," Andi quickly added. "Taffy and I jump through flaming rings, but I always stay seated."

It was best to remind Mitch that she was not trying any new riding tricks. One broken arm was enough.

"Good idea." Mitch chuckled and set to work saddling Panda and Chase, his sorrel gelding.

The sun was up and already blazing when Andi,

Mitch, and Melinda prodded their horses along the twelve-mile road to town. Andi wanted to gallop, but Mitch held her back.

"No sense arriving rumpled and sweaty," he said. "They have to unload the circus wagons from the train and line them up before the parade can even begin. We have plenty of time."

Andi slowed Taffy to a bouncy trot and edged her way back to Mitch's side. "You know lots about the circus, don't you?" Melinda's words from last Sunday swirled around in her head. "Did you really want to run away and join them?"

Mitch burst out laughing. "Melinda's been tattling on me again."

"Well, you did," Melinda said in a huff. She stuffed her blowing skirt and petticoat more securely under her legs.

"Do you still want to?" Andi held her breath. Mitch was nineteen years old and all grown up. He could do whatever he wanted. *I hope he doesn't still want to join the circus.*

Mitch shook his head. "Not anymore. Father was right to keep me home."

Andi sighed in relief. *Thank you, God!*

"But I sure wanted to back then," Mitch said. "So did all of my friends. We had never seen anything like it. The excitement of a circus made ordinary life look dull. The bright colors, the breathtaking

acrobatic tricks"—he paused and winked at Andi—
"and those clowns!"

Andi's heart skipped a beat. "What about them?"

Mitch grinned. "I dreamed of being a circus
clown, walking around on high stilts. I wanted little
kids to look up at me and *ooh* and *aah*. I didn't waste
any time nailing together a pair of stilts to practice
with."

Melinda giggled. "I remember you stumbling
around the yard on those stilts. You had bruises from
head to toe from falling so much."

"The circus left town before I got the knack of
using them," Mitch admitted.

Walking around on high stilts sounded like fun.
If Andi could figure out how to do it, she would be
taller than anybody else on the ranch. "Where are
those stilts now?" she asked.

Mitch shrugged. "In a dusty corner of the barn,
maybe."

"They've most likely been burned up as fire-
wood," Melinda said.

The rest of the way to town, Andi kept herself
busy thinking about how she could talk Mitch into
making her a pair of stilts. Before she knew it, they
were trotting down Fresno's main street.

"Look!" she squealed.

Two blocks away, huge draft horses were slowly
pulling circus wagons down the street. The parade

stretched from the railroad depot all the way past the new courthouse, headed for the large field just outside town.

Townsfolk crowded the wooden sidewalks along both sides of Tulare Street. Boys and girls dashed between the red-and-yellow baggage wagons hauling the circus tents. Jugglers tossed balls.

Buglers on white horses blew their trumpets, calling everyone to the parade. Acrobats turned cartwheels and did backward flips in the middle of the street.

"Hurry," Andi cried. "We're missing it!" She slid from Taffy's back and tugged on the reins. No time to find a hitching rail. Most looked full anyway. She broke into a run. Taffy trotted along behind, snorting.

"Hold your horses, Andi," Mitch shouted. "Wait for us."

"I *am* holding my horse!" Andi gripped Taffy's reins and squeezed through the crowd near a side street. The bystanders made way for the palomino. But they quickly filled in around Taffy, blocking Andi's view.

"I can't see," she grumbled.

No matter how hard Andi pressed against the grown-ups, they didn't budge. With all the jostling, shouting, laughing, and bugle blowing, nobody heard her either.

A firecracker exploded nearby. Taffy whinnied. Andi held on tighter.

The smothering heat made Andi pant for breath. Angry tears pricked her eyes. She'd come all this way to watch the parade, but nobody would let her wiggle to the front. She saw only dark skirts, black trousers, tall hats, and wide, floppy bonnets.

Suddenly, a strong pair of arms lifted Andi high over the heads of the blocking crowd. She gasped and let go of Taffy's reins.

"Is this better?" Mitch settled her on his shoulder.

It was much better . . . until she came face-to-face with a clown ten feet tall.

⚡ CHAPTER 3 ⚡

Circus Parade

Andi's heart raced out of control at the sight of the tall clown in his red, white, and blue Uncle Sam outfit. She wrapped her arms around Mitch's head and hung on for dear life.

"Hey, I can't see." He peeled her arms away.

"Let's go home," Andi said, trembling. She'd seen enough.

"Don't be silly," Melinda said. "You're nine years old." She stood on tiptoes, trying to catch a better view. "It's just a man on stilts under all those circus clothes."

A man on stilts, Andi told herself. *Just a man on stil—*

The clown pulled a cord. *Boing!* A painted wooden head sprang out of his hat. It bobbed up and down on a large spring until it was only inches away from Andi's face.

The crowd roared approval of the real-life jack-in-the-box.

Andi shrieked. She pitched backward off Mitch's shoulder.

A man standing behind Mitch caught Andi before she hit the ground. He set her carefully on her feet.

Mitch picked her up. "I'm sorry, Andi. I had no idea that would happen."

By the time Andi's heart slowed down, the clown was a block away. *Good riddance!*

"You girls sit up here." Mitch settled Andi onto Taffy's broad back and boosted Melinda up behind her. "Best seats for a parade."

The bystanders parted for Mitch and Taffy. He shifted the horse to the front, facing the parade. "Better now?"

Andi nodded.

Melinda slipped an arm around Andi's waist. "Don't be scared of that silly ol' clown. The best part of the parade is coming. Look!"

Andi turned to see where her sister was pointing. A wagon carrying a brass band rolled by, pulled by six high-stepping black horses. The musicians wore red, white, and blue, just like the Uncle Sam clown. "Yankee Doodle" blasted from their instruments.

Women and children atop the next wagon tossed penny candy to the crowd. While the rest of Fresno's boys and girls scrambled to pick up the sweets, Andi stared at the circus performers' children.

She nudged Melinda. "What a fun, exciting life those kids must have."

"It sure looks like it," Melinda said. She waved. "Howdy! Welcome to Fresno!"

The circus kids waved back. It was easy to see Melinda and Andi sitting up on Taffy.

Andi waved too and watched the wagonload of smiling, laughing children disappear down the street. *What fun it would be to ride the circus train, be in a parade, and learn to juggle and trick ride!*

Had her friend Sadie's father once sat up high in a circus parade and tossed candy to kids? *I'll have to ask her sometime.* Mr. Hollister was a poor sheepherder on the borders of the Circle C ranch now. *I wonder if he misses the circus.*

Melinda's soft gasp pulled Andi from her daydreaming. "Oh my goodness!"

Andi blinked and focused on the parade of horses prancing by. Sleek black horses and snow-white horses shook their flowing manes and flicked their tails. Red feathers and shiny bells decorated their bridles. Their riders were dressed in shimmering costumes—much brighter than the posters showed.

A smiling young woman came after the performers' horses. She stood with one foot on a golden palomino that could have been Taffy's twin. Her other foot balanced on the back of a white horse. She held the reins and waved to the onlookers.

Andi watched in awe. Did this ordinary-looking girl, who seemed no older than Mitch, really leap through rings of fire without burning up?

She turned to Melinda. "It's Miss Minnie Mae from the circus poster. Only"—Andi paused—"both horses were palominos in the picture. Now, one is white."

"You don't miss a thing," Melinda said. "Her palomino looks just like Taffy."

Miss Minnie Mae seemed to think so too. When she turned to wave at the people on Andi's side of the street, her eyes grew wide.

"You have a splendid-looking horse, young lady," Miss Minnie called over the commotion.

Those standing nearest to Andi turned to look at her. She beamed, speechless. The champion female bareback rider of the world was speaking to *her*.

Melinda poked her in the side. "Don't be rude. Say something."

"Thank you," Andi yelled back. "You have pretty horses too."

Miss Minnie continued to trot her horses along the street but turned her head to look back. She watched Andi and Taffy until the next circus wagon blocked her view.

The sun climbed higher, but Andi didn't notice the heat. *I met Miss Minnie Mae!* "Did you see that, Mitch? She talked to me. She likes Taffy."

Mitch nodded then looked at the clock tower. "Time's a-wastin'. If you want to come back for the show this afternoon, we need to be heading home soon."

"Not till the parade is over," Andi begged. "Oh, look! More animals."

Cory joined Andi just as another group of wagons began rolling by. He grinned up at her. "You weren't hard to find." He waved his arms. "You shoulda been there, Andi. I watched 'em unload the wagons off the flatbed cars early this morning. I even helped a circus boy water the elephants."

"The elephants!"

Talking to a world-champion bareback rider suddenly didn't seem quite so thrilling. Andi searched the dust-choked street for the elephants.

Nothing. She sighed.

"Yep," Cory said. "I poured it straight out of the water wagon and into three big tubs. Boy, elephants sure drink a lot. They suck it up with their trunks and—" He stopped and pointed. "Hey, there he is."

"Who?"

"The boy I helped this morning."

Andi followed Cory's gaze to a bright-red caged wagon. The wheels were painted with red, orange, and yellow markings. Three lions with spreading manes paced back and forth. One stopped, swiped a paw at the bars, and roared.

Andi shivered.

"Hi, Henry!" Cory shouted and waved to his new friend.

Henry sat up on the high seat next to a heavyset driver. Instead of waving back, he gripped the edges of the seat and stared straight ahead.

"That boy is mighty brave to sit on top of a cage full of wild jungle beasts," Andi said.

Cory nodded.

The big man driving the wagon nudged Henry and bent close to his ear. Henry turned and looked at Cory. He lifted his hand, gave Cory a tiny smile, and waved.

Cory sighed. "Henry's a lucky duck to live and work with the circus. Wish I was him."

Andi studied Henry's thin, dirt-streaked face. He looked nothing like the merry, candy-tossing children from earlier in the parade.

If Henry's so lucky, Andi thought, *then why doesn't he look happier?*

"Here come the elephants!"

Cory's shout turned Andi's head. He stood in the middle of the street, peering down the long line

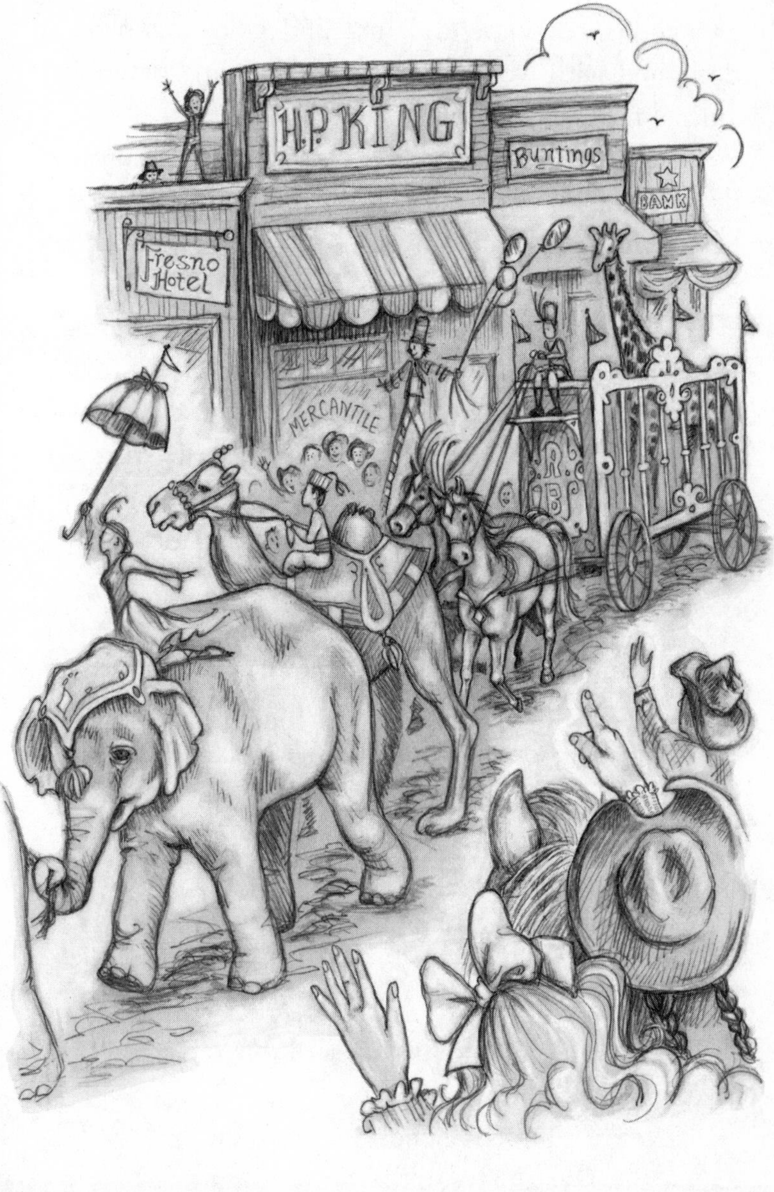
H.P. KING
Buntings
BANK
Fresno Hotel
MERCANTILE

of wagons. They were all red and gold and blue, decorated with wood carvings and brightly painted animal faces.

Then Andi saw them. Five elephants! Her mouth dropped open. A man stood on the lead elephant's head. The rest paraded by, each trunk grasping the tail in front of them.

Next, two camels plodded by. Their big, leathery foot pads sent the dust flying. Then more animal cages: monkeys, tigers, a snake wagon, and even a tall giraffe. Its neck stretched high above the wagon top.

Andi sat still as a statue and took it all in. So many wonders in one place!

Four white draft horses pulled the last wagon in the parade. Smoke poured from a stovepipe that stuck out of the roof. A man playing a keyboard sat in front. The song, "Oh, Susanna," blared from a dozen tall pipes. Steam puffed out.

Taffy laid her ears back at the noise.

"It's loud!" Andi yelled.

"It's a calliope," Mitch explained over the racket. "It makes music by pushing steam through all those shiny pipes."

When the calliope disappeared down the street, the crowd broke up.

"I've got a bunch of chores waiting for me," Cory said. "But Pa said I could see everything first. I'm going to watch the tents go up." He waved good-bye and ran off toward the field.

"I want to watch too," Andi begged.

"You'll see the show soon enough," Mitch said. "Let's go home."

Andi obeyed, but she kept looking back until she could no longer see the people scurrying around the circus grounds.

⊰ CHAPTER 4 ⊱

Circus Boy

Andi and Melinda talked all during lunch. The few times Mitch tried to get a word in edgewise, the girls cut him off.

"No, let me tell!" Andi said.

"Wait, Mitch. There were five tigers, not four," Melinda corrected him.

Chad rolled his eyes and leaned back in his chair. "What happened to the mealtime rule that says children should be seen and not heard? The girls are chattering louder than a cageful of monkeys."

Mother laughed. "When a circus comes to town, some rules can't help but be broken." She smiled. "Finish your lunch, girls. We need to hurry if we want to find good seats at this afternoon's performance."

Andi rushed through her meal. She tried not to wiggle when Melinda buttoned up the back of her Sunday dress. "I hope the circus is worth all this dressing up for," she grumbled.

Long puffed sleeves. Scratchy lace trim. She pulled at the tight collar and winced.

Mother brushed Andi's hair, re-braided it, and tied fresh ribbons. "Don't fuss. Everyone will be dressed in their best. A circus is a very special event."

"Must be near as important as Sunday school," Andi whispered to Melinda when they climbed into the surrey's back seat.

"Andrea Rose Carter!" Melinda sat down hard. She clapped her hand over Andi's mouth. "You mustn't say such things. A circus, as important as going to church to worship God? Shame on you. Don't let Mother hear."

Andi peeled Melinda's fingers away. "If it's not as important, then why do I have to dress up like this? Why can't I be comfortable and wear an everyday dress to the circus?"

Melinda didn't answer, which meant she didn't know.

Justin helped Mother into the surrey then climbed up beside her to drive. Andi expected Justin to dress up. He wore his good suit and tie every day when he went to his lawyer office in town.

But Andi did not expect to see Chad and Mitch

in their Sunday suits sitting up on the ranch's dirty work wagon. She burst out laughing. "You two look silly up there in your fancy clothes."

"We're picking up supplies after the show," Chad snapped. "Any other questions?"

Muffling her giggles, Andi shook her head. Poor Chad. In his stuffy suit coat and string tie he looked unhappier than a roped calf.

The hour-long trip to town flew by. Justin dropped everyone off at the circus grounds and left to find a place for the surrey. Chad dropped off Mitch and did the same with the wagon.

Andi whirled to take everything in. A few hours ago, this field had stood brown and empty. Now it was transformed into a magical world. Everywhere Andi looked, circus tents of all sizes, shapes, and colors stood waiting to be explored.

She sniffed. A mixture of earthy animal odors hit her. It smelled like the ranch, only stronger. "What can we look at while we're waiting for the show to start?" she asked.

"How about this?" Mitch pointed to a big tent behind the ticket wagon. The sign read **WILD ANIMAL MENAGERIE**. "It's five cents to see them up close. Mother and Justin will save us seats."

Mitch dropped a nickel into Andi's outstretched hand and another into Melinda's. They hurried around to the entrance.

Cory stood fidgeting just outside the canvas door. "Hey, Andi. You going inside?"

She nodded. "How about you?"

"Nah." He shrugged and kicked at the ground with the toe of his shoe. "I don't have a nickel and—"

"You do now." Mitch flicked Cory a coin. "Come with us."

Cory's eyes lit up. "Thanks, Mitch!"

A circus worker took their money and raised the flap. The four of them ducked inside.

Andi looked around. The caged wagons formed two long rows along the sides of the tent. Animal noises pounded Andi's ears—squealing, chattering, growling.

It's louder than a calliope in here. And it's so hot! It stinks too.

The town's ladies held perfume-scented hankies to their noses. So did Melinda.

Andi didn't bother. She and Cory darted from cage to cage, *oohing* and *aahing* at the wild beasts. Lions and tigers. A boa constrictor twelve feet long. Monkeys. A giraffe whose head nearly touched the ceiling.

Across the walkway, two elephants chomped hay.

One cage held a giant tub of water. Two sea lions swam and barked. Andi got a flipper full of water in her face when she and Cory stepped too close. A circus worker laughed.

Andi didn't. She wiped her face and went back to the monkeys. "The monkeys and apes are my favorites," she told Cory, pressing closer to the ape cage.

Just then, a curious baby chimpanzee poked his hand through the bars. He grabbed Andi's braid and yanked.

Andi yelped. "Let go!" She yanked back.

The chimp screeched and jumped up and down, tugging on Andi's long braid.

Andi shrieked and pulled harder. Finally, her braid slipped through the chimp's fingers. She jumped back, panting.

The visitors and workers laughed. Mitch grinned and pointed to the cage.

"My ribbon!" Andi shouted, furious.

The chimp waved the blue hair ribbon, turned a somersault, and howled his victory.

The bystanders laughed harder. "Was that part of the show?" a boy asked.

Red-faced, Andi dashed to the exit at the other side of the tent. *I don't want to be part of any chimpanzee tug-of-war act.* She ducked through the canvas flap and—

Oof!

Andi crashed into a small boy. They tumbled to the ground in a heap. *That hurt!* She rubbed her shoulder and scooted away.

The boy sat up. He was hatless and dressed in

a clean but too-big red-and-white jacket. A wooden tray dangled from a strap hanging from one shoulder.

Andi stared at him. The lion-cage boy!

"Watch where you're going," Cory yelled at the boy. Then he stopped. "Henry? Is that you?"

Mitch stepped up and raised Henry to his feet. "No harm done."

Melinda helped Andi. "I can't believe it," she muttered. "Dusty and soiled as usual." She brushed the dirt from Andi's dress. "Are you hurt?"

Andi shook herself free. "I'm fine." She looked at Henry. "You all right?"

"So sorry, miss." Henry flushed bright-red. "Please don't tell Truckee I dirtied your pretty dress. He already thinks I'm the clumsiest boy that ever lived." He bent over to pick up the tray. His hands shook.

"Who's Truckee?" Andi asked.

Henry lifted the wooden tray and slipped the long strap over his head. "Truckee's my boss. He runs the candy counter." He tapped the tray. "I sell peanuts, candy, and lemonade during the show."

He pointed to a wagon parked between two tents. "That's him way over there."

A bald man with a drooping moustache stood at his circus stand, filling glasses with lemonade. When he glanced up, Henry hid behind Mitch. The man frowned and turned his head back and forth as if he were searching for someone.

He was probably trying to find Henry. "He looks mean and grumpy," Andi said.

"You don't know the half of it." Henry sighed. "Truckee's mean as they come."

"Why do your folks let him boss you like that?" Cory asked.

Henry bowed his head. "Don't got any folks. Just an aunt and uncle in Missouri."

Andi bit her lip. Missouri was a long way from California. What was a little boy like Henry doing so far from home? "You don't look any older than seven or eight. Why are you—"

"Henry!"

The boy jumped at Truckee's bellow.

"Henry Jackson! Where did you sneak off to now? You lazy boy! Show yourself."

Henry took a deep breath. "I gotta go before Truckee sees me with you." He glanced around, picked up his cap, and put it on. "You won't tell him I knocked you down, will you?"

Andi shook her head. Her throat was too tight to speak. She stared at Henry as he turned and ran off. Then she looked at Mitch.

Mitch nodded. "Yes, Andi. I think Henry might be a runaway."

CHAPTER 5

Under the Big Top

Andi watched Henry scurry back to the candy seller.

Truckee hit the little boy then began filling his tray with glasses of lemonade and small red-and-white striped bags. Henry sagged under the weight.

Cory stepped up beside Andi. "I guess running away to join the circus isn't all fun and games," he said quietly. "Maybe Henry's not a lucky duck."

Andi was thinking the same thing.

Just then, lively music began to fill the air, calling people to the afternoon performance. Mitch herded Andi and Melinda toward the big top—the largest circus tent, right in the middle of the grounds.

"Are you coming?" he asked Cory.

Cory shook his head. "We're going to the evening

performance. Pa told me I've got four stalls to muck out to pay my way. Bye, Andi!" He darted into the crowd and out of sight.

Mitch already had their tickets, so there was no need to stop by the red ticket wagon.

Good thing. A dozen people stood in line. They no doubt hoped to buy a seat before the afternoon show sold out.

Andi walked into the big top and stopped. It took a minute for her eyes to adjust to the dim light. When they did, she tried to see everything at once.

A sawdust track circled all the way around two big rings in the middle of the tent. A two-foot-high canvas barricade separated the performance area from where people were finding their seats in the stands.

An iron cage with three lions inside took up one ring. High up in the other ring, Andi saw platforms with swings attached. A tightwire stretched between the poles that held up the tent.

"Somebody is going to walk across that wire," Melinda said, grinning. "You just watch and see."

Andi planned to. But how could she see it all? Each ring showed a different part of the show. If she watched the trapeze artists in one ring, she might miss the world-champion bareback rider leaping through a ring of fire. Or the lion tamer and his savage jungle—

44

"There they are," Mitch said. He prodded Andi. "Get a move on. We're holding up the parade."

Andi's family sat in the front row right between the two rings. Andi squeezed in next to Justin and Mother and sat down. From here, she had the best view of both rings.

At least, if my eyes can go back and forth quick enough.

Straight across from Andi, on the other side of the big top, the brass band played happy, toe-tapping tunes. The crowd poured into the tent and found their seats.

"These are good spots," Andi told Mother. "I can see everything."

Chad peeked around Justin. "There's a fine view of the clowns too." He pointed to a group of figures somersaulting around the track. Tiny dogs dressed in costumes ran next to the clowns, yipping and doing silly tricks.

Andi's heart thumped. *They're coming closer!*

"Chad," Mother warned.

Andi looked around for the ten-foot-tall, jack-in-the-box clown, but he was nowhere in sight. She relaxed.

The clowns tripped and tumbled and acted so silly that Andi was soon laughing along with the rest of the people in the audience. *They're not scary at all*, she realized. When a clown pulled a flower out of thin air and handed it to Andi, she took it without flinching.

Jugglers followed the clowns around the track. They came so close to the canvas barrier that Andi could almost touch them. She watched, wide-eyed, as they juggled oranges, bowling pins, and knives.

One juggler stopped right in front of Andi. Someone lit three torches. The juggler tossed them into the air. A clown threw him a fourth flaming torch. Then a fifth . . . a sixth . . . a seventh!

Andi could feel the heat. *What if he drops a torch?* She covered her eyes. *I can't watch!*

She peeked between her fingers, but the juggler did not drop even one torch. She clapped and hollered when he continued his act around the big top.

"Ladies and gentlemen! Boys and girls!"

A tall man in white pants and a bright-red jacket and hat ran out and stood between the two rings. The music stopped. A hush fell over the crowd.

"Welcome to an exhibition without equal on the face of the earth," the ringmaster shouted. He pointed to Andi's left. "In this ring you will be dazzled by the daring and death-defying feats of the Flying Robinson Family, trapeze artists of worldwide fame."

He waved toward the opposite ring. "Here I call your attention to the fearless Clyde Bates, lion tamer and master of the savage jungle beasts."

As if on cue, one of the lions gave a mighty roar. The crowd gasped.

The ringmaster waved his arms. "So now, with no further ado, I present to you Coleman's American Circus!" He dashed away.

Then everything happened at once.

Andi could barely keep up. Her gaze shot to the high fliers in the far ring. To the lion tamer trapped behind bars with the growling lions. Back and forth. Acrobats. Lions.

A few minutes later, an elephant replaced the lion act. A tiger and his trainer entered. There was no cage. A rope leash encircled the tiger's neck.

Andi grabbed Mother's hand. "What keeps the tiger from chewing away his leash? Why doesn't he claw his trainer?"

"He's well trained." Mother squeezed Andi's hand. "Don't worry."

Andi didn't have time to worry. There was too much to see. The tiger leaped onto the elephant's back. Around and around the ring they went.

Later, a family of bicyclists circled the ring doing tricks. A tiny child stood on his father's shoulders as he peddled from high up on the huge front bicycle wheel.

Each performance left Andi breathless.

"Peanuts, candy, lemonade! It's cold. It's fresh. Only five cents a glass."

Andi whirled at Henry's loud words. She pulled her attention away from Miss Minnie Mae, world-champion bareback rider, to see the boy standing in front of the crowd. Half his tray held glass tumblers of lemonade. The other half displayed bags of snacks.

"Only five cents! Get your nice, cold lemonade. Peanuts. Chewing gum. Candy."

Andi tugged on Justin's sleeve. "Can I have some peanuts? And lemonade too?"

"May I," Mother corrected.

"May I?" Andi said. "Please? Before he goes by."

Justin motioned to Henry.

Grinning, the little boy hurried over. "Peanuts, miss?"

"Yes, please," Andi said. "And lemonade."

"Coming right up." Henry sorted through the striped bags and found an extra-full one. He passed Andi the peanuts then carefully handed her a glass of lemonade.

Melinda bought chewing gum, and Mitch asked for peppermints.

"Twenty cents," Henry said.

Justin gave him a quarter.

Henry carefully counted five pennies into Justin's hand. Then he shifted the heavy tray, adjusted the strap on his shoulders, and took off, calling into the stands. He made a few more sales then moved on.

Andi cracked open her peanuts and watched Miss

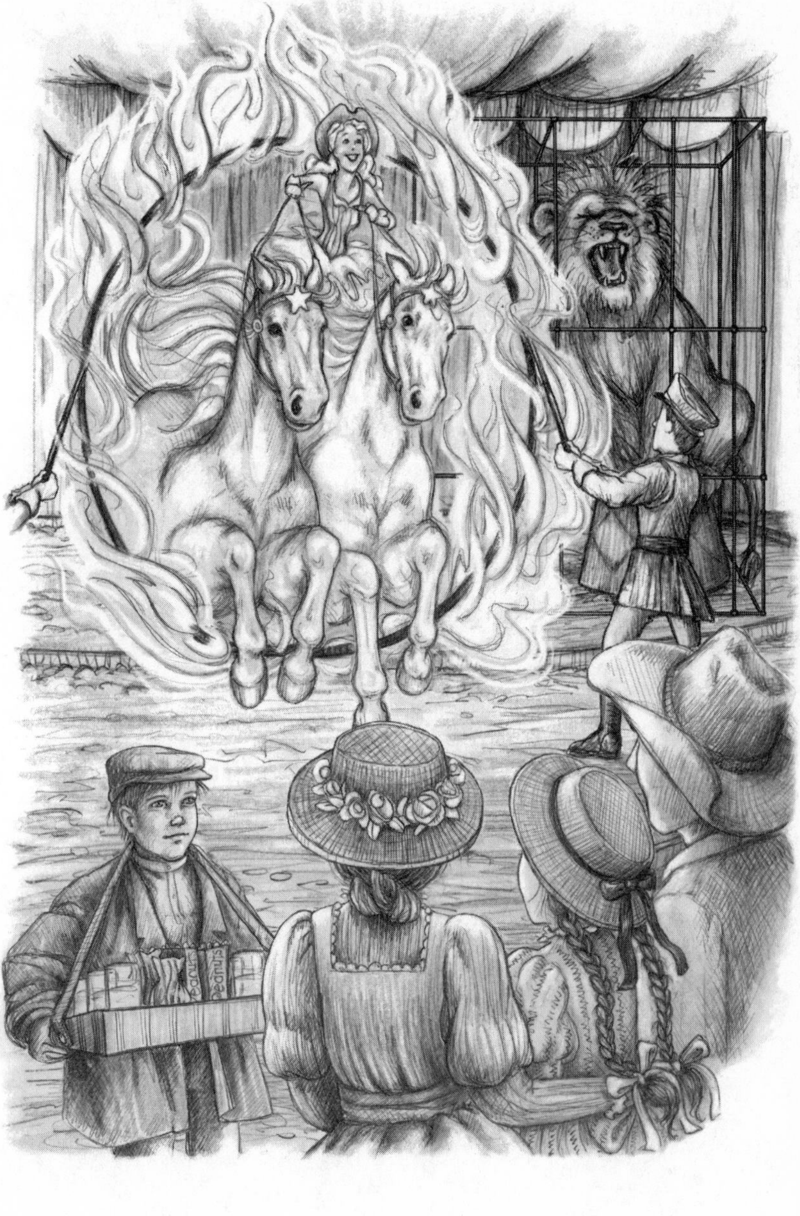
peanuts

Minnie Mae perform riding tricks. Each stunt looked more amazing than the last. For her final act, she took her pair of horses—one golden and one white—through the ring of fire.

Andi held her breath. She imagined the golden horse as Taffy. She pictured herself as Miss Minnie. *Miss Andrea Rose and her world-famous palomino dazzle the crowds with their—*

Roaring applause shattered Andi's daydream. She set down her peanuts and lemonade and clapped loud and long.

When the clapping ended, Andi settled herself for the next act. To her surprise, Henry hurried toward her. He took off his tray and lowered it to the ground. Clenching one fist, he scanned the rows of people behind the Carters.

She turned to watch.

"Hey, mister!" Henry hollered to a rough-looking man four rows up. He held up his fist. "This ten-cent piece you gave me is bad. Please. Give me a good one."

When the man didn't answer, Henry started to climb into the stands.

⊰ CHAPTER 6 ⊱

Ten Cents' Worth of Trouble

Andi twisted around to get a better view. Red-faced and shaking, Henry made his way up the tightly packed bench seats.

A woman yelped. Another tried to shoo Henry away. One man said a bad word and told the boy to get lost.

Henry ignored them and kept climbing.

A father picked up his little girl and sat her in his lap for safekeeping. Henry crawled into the empty spot. He carefully stood up to face the man on the next row up. "Please, mister. I gotta give you this lead dime back. Give me a good—"

"Out of my way, boy." The man glared at Henry as if he were a bug that needed squashing. "How can I see the show with you standing in front of me?"

Andi's heart pounded. The scene in the stands was scarier than watching the lions try to eat the lion tamer. At least the jungle beasts were kept in an iron cage in the middle of the circus ring. This angry man was only four rows away.

Henry did not back down. He stood up straight with his arms stiff at his sides. "You'll like the show a lot better if you give me another dime."

The man snorted. "Get along with you now." He pushed Henry to one side and focused on the act in the far ring.

Henry tried again. "Please, mister. Won't you please give me the money back? Truckee's awful mad. He'll fix me good if I don't get it back. You know it was bad money you gave me."

"I don't know anything about it," the man growled. "Get out of here before I drop you between the seats."

What a mean, horrible man to cheat Henry, Andi thought.

Other people must have thought so too. A lady sitting three seats away from the cheater scowled at the man but didn't say anything. She looked frightened of his angry face and loud voice.

"Aw, George, give him the lousy dime," the man seated next to him said.

Mean George crossed his arms over his chest. "I didn't give him bad money. These circus kids always find a way to cheat the audience. This is just one more trick." He laughed. "Besides, even if I did give him a dud, he can't prove nothin'."

George waved a hand in Henry's face. "Go on! Find somebody else to pester. You won't get nothin' from me."

Wearing a long face, Henry turned and started making his way down the board seats. Tears pooled in his eyes, but he brushed them away with his sleeve. He stumbled, caught himself, and stepped down a row.

His foot landed on a lady's skirt.

"Watch where you're stepping, you clumsy little boy." The woman yanked the folds of fabric out from under his shoe.

Henry lost his footing and fell forward. Arms outstretched to catch himself, he plowed right into Melinda.

Thud! They both landed on the sawdust ground.

Andi gasped. If Melinda had been paying attention, she might have caught the boy. After all, she was much bigger than Henry. But Melinda's eyes had been glued to the circus performance. She never had a chance.

Poor Henry, Andi thought. *Maybe he really is the clumsiest boy who ever lived.*

"What in the world?" Chad yanked Henry up. "What's got into you, boy?"

Mitch settled a dazed Melinda back onto her seat. He pulled out his bandana and wiped the sawdust from her face. Then he brushed off her clothes.

Henry was trembling. "I'm awful sorry, m-miss. I didn't mean no harm. I—" He burst into tears, cutting off whatever he planned to say next.

Mother took the little boy's hand and drew him next to her. "It's all right. You're not in any trouble. Tell me what's wrong."

Henry shook his head. No words came out.

"I'll tell you what's wrong," Andi said. "While you were all watching the act, Henry was up there trying to get his money back." She pointed to the rough man four rows away. "He gave Henry a lead dime instead of a real one."

"Is that true?" Mother asked gently. "Did that man cheat you?"

Henry nodded and bowed his head. "Yes'm. Truckee told me to get it back *or else*, but the man won't make it right."

He opened his fist and showed Mother a thin, round piece of metal. Andi leaned over to get a better look.

"Well, why did you wait so long?" Chad wanted to know. "Why didn't you ask for it back right away?"

"It all happened so fast. He yelled when I didn't give him his change fast enough. So I hurried.

And . . ." He sniffed. "I don't know much about money. I always give it to Truckee."

Henry might not know about bad money, but Andi did. She recognized the piece in Henry's hand right away. One Sunday a few weeks ago when she had dropped her pennies in the offering plate she saw a dark coin mixed in with the rest of the money.

Mitch had seen it too. He'd fished it out and replaced it with a real dime. Then he slipped the lead coin into Andi's hand and whispered, "I can't believe somebody would cheat God."

Cheat God? Andi was so shocked that she'd stared at the pretend coin during the entire church service. She kept it in her treasure box so she would never forget what a lead dime looked like.

The coin in Henry's palm looked just like the one in her treasure box.

"How do you know it was that man up there?" Mother asked. She shook out her hankie and wiped the tears from Henry's thin face.

"He's the only one that gave me a dime, ma'am. The others paid in pennies and nickels." He jerked his chin toward Justin. "And he gave me a quarter."

Chad turned and eyed George. "Cheating a little boy, eh?" His eyes narrowed.

Andi held her breath. Big brother Chad might be mean and bossy at times, but he was always fair—no matter how many times she thought he wasn't.

She knew nothing annoyed Chad more than unfairness, especially if it included a bully. Especially a grown-up bully cheating a little boy. *You better watch out, Mean George!*

Chad rose from his seat. "We'll see about getting your dime back, boy. That fella's going to wish he'd never—"

"Easy, little brother." Justin closed his hand around Chad's arm. "No sense getting thrown out of here for causing a commotion. Simmer down." He tugged. "We're missing the show."

Chad sat down hard. He didn't look happy. "I don't recognize him, and I know everybody in Fresno." He shifted in his seat and muttered, "Most likely a troublemaker from that new town up north."

Justin poked around in his pocket and brought out two dimes. He took the bad coin from Henry and tossed it aside. Then he dropped the new dime in its place. "Here's ten cents so you don't get in trouble with your boss."

Henry's eyes widened.

"And here's another dime for your pocket," Justin said. "You don't need to give Truckee this one." He winked. "It's your very own. Call it a tip for doing a good job."

"Oh, thank you, sir! I won't be forgetting this. You're a real gentleman."

Henry slipped one dime into his left pocket and the other into his right. He picked up his tray.

Justin helped adjust the strap. "Better get back to work, young fella. The show's half over."

"Yes, sir." Henry bobbed his head and went on his way. "Peanuts! Candy! Lemonade! It's cold. It's fresh. Only five cents a glass."

"He seems like a nice little boy," Mother said. "Do you know him, Andrea?"

Andi nodded. "I met him just before the show. His name's Henry. He's a runa—"

"Look!" A boy's loud cry from nearby jerked Andi back to the performance. Five elephants, trunk to tail, were parading into the ring.

Andi swallowed what she planned to tell Mother. The elephants took up her whole attention.

Besides, Andi didn't know for sure Henry had run away to join the circus. Mitch was only guessing.

And maybe Henry wanted to keep it a secret.

CHAPTER 7

Henry's Invitation

Andi left the big top two hours later full of peanuts and lemonade. Sweat trickled down the back of her neck, and she fanned her face. It didn't help. The afternoon was no cooler outside than inside.

"What was your favorite act?" Justin asked as they walked through the circus grounds. "I sure enjoyed watching those bicyclists."

Visions of elephants, lions, bareback riders, and acrobats danced inside Andi's head. How could she choose a favorite?

"I know which act was *my* favorite," Melinda said before Andi could answer. She clasped her hands together and sang, *"'He'd fly through the air with the greatest of ease, that daring young man on the flying trapeze . . .'"*

Humming, Melinda took a few dance steps.

Chad shook his head. Mitch laughed.

Andi rolled her eyes at her sister's dreamy look. The Robinson boy had flown through the air just like the man in the song. He didn't look much older than Melinda, but he was an excellent acrobat. Andi had held her breath when he let go of the trapeze and grabbed his father's ankles in midair.

A sudden thought took Andi's breath away. Melinda was fourteen, the same age Mitch was when he wanted to join the circus. "Mother," she said, "don't let Melinda run away on account of a trapeze artist."

Melinda stopped humming. She put her hands on her hips and frowned. "I wouldn't do such a silly thing. But I can admire Stewart Robinson, can't I?"

"I guess." Andi shrugged then brightened. "My favorite act was when Miss Minnie Mae and her two horses leaped through the ring of fire." She turned to Mitch. "Did you see it? Neither horse even twitched."

"Of course I saw it," Mitch said. "I was sitting right there."

"You might have been watching the tightrope walker in the other ring." Andi knew how quickly someone could miss the best part of an act. She'd blinked one time and missed a triple somersault in the air.

"It was a good act," Melinda agreed. "But I wonder why Miss Mae's horses aren't a matched pair like the other riders' horses. Why not two white horses? Or two black ones? Or two palominos like the poster advertised?"

Andi wondered the same thing. "One of the palominos might have hurt his leg."

"True," Melinda said thoughtfully.

Andi sighed. That would be too bad. Matching palominos would look mighty fine together, shining like gold against the fiery ring.

For a moment, Andi pictured herself on Taffy, riding next to Miss Minnie Mae. *Can two people go through the ring at the same time?*

Andi pushed her wishful thinking aside just as Chad said good-bye.

"Mitch and I are off to find the wagon and load up our supplies. We'll meet you for supper at the hotel around six." He grinned at Mother's questioning look. "We'll try to keep from ruining our clothes."

When Chad and Mitch left, the rest of the family wandered around the circus grounds. Truckee stood behind his candy counter, shouting out the quality of his goods. A small line formed. Henry was nowhere in sight.

"Hey, Andi!" Cory waved and dashed over, panting. "I've just been to a sideshow. Pa gave me a nickel, and you won't believe what I saw! A sword

61

swallower. He didn't swallow only one sword. He swallowed *three*. All the way down his throat and back up again."

Andi gasped. "Without cutting himself?"

"Yep. And there was a giant rat—the biggest in the world. Leastways, that's what the sign said. Then I saw a two-headed calf. Really, Andi. It had two heads. It was alive and everything."

Andi's mouth fell open.

"I saw a little man too," Cory said. "He wasn't more'n two feet high and only came up to here." He held his hand waist high. "They called him a midget." Cory stopped for breath. "How was the show?"

Andi shared the thrills Cory would see tonight under the big top, but inside she itched to see the sideshow. *A two-headed calf?* She shivered.

"For goodness' sake, Cory Blake," Melinda said. "I don't know why you want to see such freaks of nature. I wouldn't pay a penny to see them, much less a whole nickel."

Melinda glanced at the tent with a sign above the canvas door. **SIDESHOW 5 CENTS**, it said. "I wouldn't go inside that tent even if they paid me. It's indecent."

I would.

Andi plucked Justin's sleeve. "May I have a nickel to see the sideshow? It sounds—"

"No, Andrea," Mother broke in. "There are some

things that are best left alone. Especially for little girls."

Andi opened her mouth to argue, but Mother had more to say.

"Your imagination does not need any help. The circus performance today was more than enough excitement. I don't want you to wake up tonight with another bad dream."

"Yes, ma'am." Andi felt her face redden.

A few nights ago, savage jungle animals from the circus posters had chased Andi right out of her bed and into Mother's. It was the first time since last spring's crashing thunderstorm that Andi had been too scared to sleep in her own room.

Perhaps Mother knew best, after all.

Just then, Henry rounded the corner of the big top. He gave Andi a wide smile. "I was hoping you didn't rush off after the show."

"We're having supper at the hotel," Andi told him. "So we're staying in town for a while."

"That's good," Henry said. "'Cuz I got an idea. I get a break until this evening's performance. And I don't have to wash lemonade glasses for another hour." He leaned closer. "Wanna see behind the scenes?"

Andi wrinkled her forehead. "What does that mean?"

"I want to show you the places where circus goers

aren't usually allowed. Maybe even meet some of the performers."

Melinda caught her breath. "You can do that?"

"I got a few friends here," Henry explained. "When they heard what you did for me, they invited you to have a look around."

"May we, Mother?" Melinda's eyes gleamed.

Andi giggled. "You just want to meet that young trapeze artist."

Melinda elbowed her. "Hush." Her cheeks turned red.

"It sounds like a wonderful opportunity," Mother agreed. "Thank you, Henry. It's very kind of you."

Henry shook his head. "No, ma'am. You're the kind ones." He turned and headed for an enclosed area behind the big top. "Come on! I only got an hour."

⊰ CHAPTER 8 ⊱

Behind the Scenes

Andi forgot about the sideshow. A tour of the places normally off-limits to ordinary folks was sure to be more exciting than seeing a two-headed calf. She skipped away to join Henry.

Justin pulled her back. "Hold your horses, honey. We need to make plans. I don't care to see behind the scenes, and Mother is feeling the heat. I'm taking her to my office to rest until supper."

Andi slumped. "Mother said we could go."

"You may," Mother said. "But you girls must stay together at all times."

That was easy. Andi knew Melinda wanted to see behind the scenes as much as she did.

"Come over to my office at six," Justin said. "Not a minute later."

"Yes, sir," Andi and Melinda said together.

Andi glanced over her shoulder. Henry and Cory walked side by side toward a high canvas fence on the other side of the grounds. They were chatting like best friends.

"Mother, Henry's leaving. May we go now?"

Mother nodded.

Andi grabbed her sister's hand and tugged. "Hurry, Melinda!"

"Six o'clock!" Justin called after them.

For once, Melinda did not have to be dragged. She ran faster than Andi to catch up with the boys.

Andi giggled. *She really wants to meet that Robinson acrobat.*

Who else might they meet? Miss Minnie Mae, the champion bareback rider? Maybe Andi could ask her what happened to the other palomino.

They caught up with Henry and Cory just outside a curtained area. A circus guard lifted part of the curtain and shooed them under it. "Make it quick."

Andi walked into a huge space surrounded by tents of all sizes. Some tents looked closed up tight. The sides of other tents had been rolled up to let the breeze in.

"These are the performers' living quarters," Henry explained. He pointed to a large tent with a stovepipe poking out through the top. "That's the cook tent, where we eat." He hurried toward another huge rectangular tent that had only three walls. The fourth side was completely open. "This is the practice tent."

Just inside, three children were gathered around a tightwire set a couple feet off the ground. One little girl raised her hand and waved. "Hi, Henry!" She climbed onto the wire and took several dainty steps.

"Hi, Sylvia," Henry replied. "These are the friends I told you about."

Sylvia hopped down and came over. "Would you like to try walking on the wire?" she asked Andi.

Walk on a wire? Like a real tightrope artist? Andi's mouth felt full of cotton, but she nodded.

Even with Sylvia holding her hand, Andi wobbled back and forth. The wire wouldn't hold still. After two steps she hit the ground. *Oof!*

Andi looked up. The wire just brushed the top of her head. The tightrope under the big top stretched much, *much* higher. If Sylvia fell from that high up, she could be killed, even if there was a net to catch her.

Andi gulped. *The circus is not for me.*

Cory didn't do any better.

Only Henry could walk all the way across. "Lots of practice," he explained when Andi clapped.

Stewart Robinson walked inside chewing on a licorice stick. He smiled at Melinda and introduced himself.

Melinda clasped her hands behind her back. "Nice

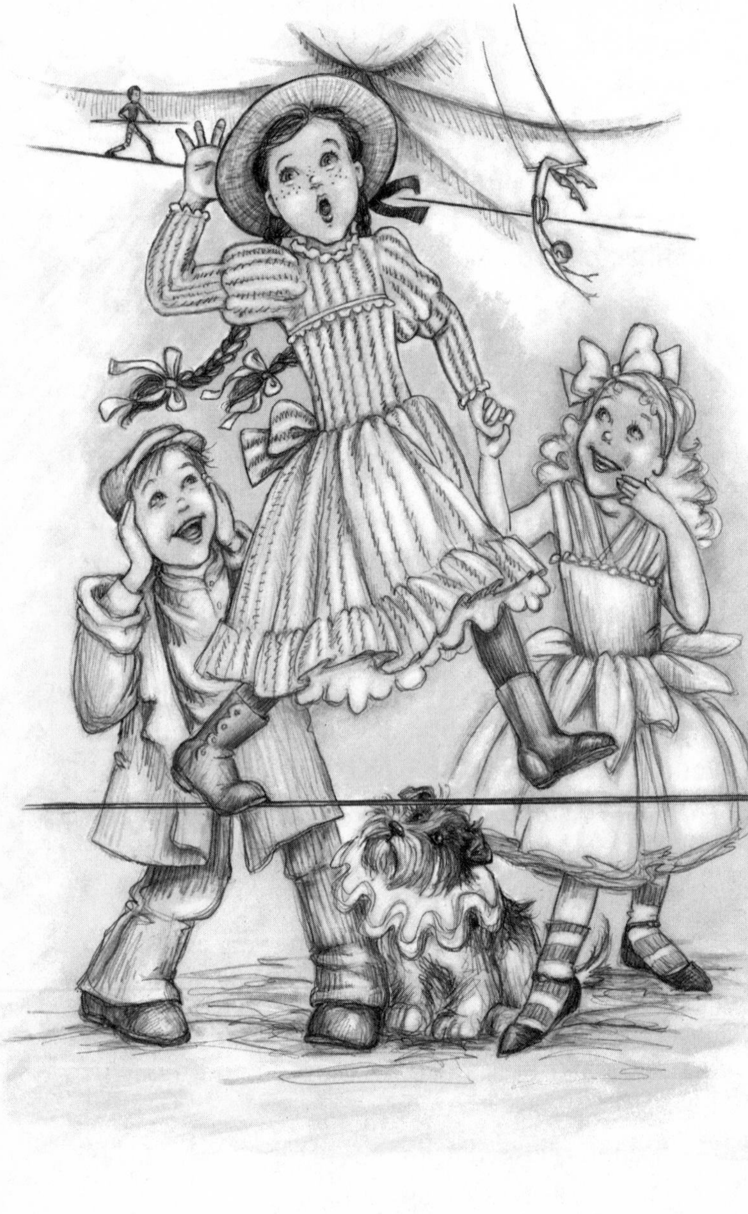

to meet you," she said shyly. She blushed and didn't say anything else. Wide-eyed, she watched Stewart run back and forth on the practice wire.

Andi shook her head. *I hope I don't act that silly when I'm fourteen.*

Two clowns without their wigs and costumes wandered past the tent's open side. A third clown climbed up on a pair of stilts and walked around the yard. Without his Uncle Sam outfit, he looked like an ordinary man on stilts.

Andi smiled. *Like Mitch!*

A new thought went through Andi's head. Daring trapeze artists were everyday people who wore sparkly outfits. They worked in a circus, and they practiced hard to be the best they could be.

Just like I have to practice to throw a lasso.

She found Henry, who had left the practice tent. He stood watching the clowns. "I didn't know everybody spent so much time practicing," Andi said.

"Over and over." Henry rolled his eyes. "Same thing all day long. I'm sick of it."

Andi caught her breath. "Then why . . ." She stopped. It was not polite to be nosy.

"Why did I join the circus?"

Andi nodded. "You don't have to tell me. Not if it's a secret."

Henry sighed, a long, sad, little-boy sigh. "Ma and Pa died of the fever last winter. My grandparents were too old to take care of me, so I went to live with Aunt Myrtle and Uncle Hank." He made a face. "On their farm."

Andi scuffed the dirt. So far, Henry hadn't said anything about the circus.

"I'm a city boy," Henry went on. "I don't know anything about farming. Uncle Hank tossed me up on his plow horse and told me to get to work. I didn't like riding around the field all day long."

"Why not?" Andi's eyebrows rose. What was more fun than riding a horse?

"I don't know." Henry shook his head. "Wish I was riding that ol' plow horse right this minute." Tears filled his eyes. "When the circus came to town, I ran off."

"Just like that?"

"Yep." He shrugged. "It was fun at first. Watering the elephants. Feeding the monkeys. Riding up on a wagon during a parade. Truckee gave me a job. Said I could earn my own money. Never had any money before, so that sounded swell."

He swiped at his tears. "Then everything changed. Once we got so far away that I couldn't run home, Truckee turned mean. He hit me when I didn't do something fast enough."

Henry started crying. "There isn't a boy in any Sunday school who's half so sorry as me. I want to go home. I don't want to stay here another minute."

Andi remembered the colorful circus posters. She thought of her own thrill when she saw the glittery costumes and daring acts. *I think maybe those posters don't tell the truth—at least not the whole truth.*

"Why don't you just go home then?" she asked.

"I can't. It costs heaps of money to go all the way back to Jefferson City. I'm supposed to get a dollar a week, but most times Truckee forgets. I asked him once, and he said I don't need any money. I get food and a place to sleep, and that's plenty."

Andi's head spun. Henry was stuck worse than if he'd stepped in thick mud.

"Truckee told me to stop bellyaching. Said I was lucky to be with the circus. Any boy would trade places with me." Henry wiped a sleeve across his nose. "They wouldn't. Not if they knew what I know."

"Do your aunt and uncle know where you are?" Andi whispered.

"I don't know. Maybe not." Henry paused. "'Cuz if they knew, wouldn't they come after me? I mean, if they really cared about me?"

Andi didn't answer. Mitch had almost joined the circus, but Father kept him from running off. If he hadn't, Mitch might have been just as stuck as Henry.

Far away from home. All alone. With no way to get back.

Andi shook inside at such a scary thought. *Please, Jesus. There must be some way to help Henry get home.*

But no ideas for helping him came to Andi's mind.

Henry glanced around then sucked in a deep breath and rubbed away the rest of his tears. He straightened his shoulders. "Don't let on I told you anything," he whispered. "Truckee will tan me good for whining. I'll be worse off than before."

Andi nodded wordlessly. Henry's secret was safe with her.

At least until she could talk to Mother.

⊰ CHAPTER 9 ⊱

Taffy's Twin

The sound of loud, friendly whinnies caught Andi's attention. She peeked past Henry. Miss Minnie Mae had come by with her horses.

Andi and Henry hurried over to where Cory and Melinda stood with Miss Mae just outside the practice tent. She wore a blue cape tied around her neck. It was trimmed with shiny-gold sequins and hung past her knees.

She looks like a princess, Andi thought. *Miss Minnie Mae, champion bareback rider of the world.* Prickles raced up and down Andi's arms. *And I get to meet her!*

"Thank you very much," Miss Mae was saying. "I'm so pleased you enjoyed the show." She kissed the palomino's nose. "Of course, I couldn't perform without Corona. He's the real star."

The second horse snorted and laid his ears back.

Miss Mae laughed. "Yes, so are you, Jupiter." She brushed his snow-white nose with her lips.

Henry greeted the bareback rider with a quick hug then stepped back. "This is Andi. Her family kept me out of trouble with Truckee today."

Miss Mae stretched out a slim, pale hand. "It's very nice to meet you. I heard about your family's kindness."

Andi shook the young woman's hand, but she couldn't keep her eyes off Corona. He was a gelding, but in every other way the palomino looked just like Taffy.

The same white blaze on his nose. Four identical white socks. His body the exact shade of gold. The same light-cream mane and tail.

Cory whistled. "Corona could be Taffy's twin, Andi."

"I know."

Miss Mae dropped Andi's hand. "You're the little girl from this morning's street parade. I thought I recognized you." She knelt down. "How old is your palomino?"

"Taffy's three."

"Splendid! Corona is five. Young horses are so much easier to train." Miss Mae rose. "You may pet him if you like. Corona loves attention."

Andi reached out and stroked the palomino's soft nose. He returned her touch by snuffling her hair.

Just like Taffy.

Melinda scratched behind Jupiter's ears. "How do you teach the horses to jump through a ring of fire?"

"Aren't you afraid they'll scorch their manes?" Cory burst out.

Andi peered at Corona's mane. Not one creamy hair looked black.

"Horses are naturally afraid of fire," Miss Mae said. "So it takes time and patience. We train them for many weeks." She patted the white horse's neck. "Jupiter had to learn faster, but he's coming along."

The matched palominos from the circus poster loosened Andi's tongue. "What happened to the other palomino? The one on the poster?"

Miss Mae sighed. "I often wonder if people notice that. Luna became ill and died last month."

"I'm sorry," Melinda said. "I can't imagine losing my horse, Panda."

Andi couldn't imagine losing Taffy. Poor Miss Mae!

"Mr. Coleman—the circus owner—is looking for a new horse," Miss Mae said. "A matched pair is part of the act's appeal." She shook her head. "So far he's had no luck. Until he finds a new palomino, Jupiter has to fill in."

Andi shook her head. "It's not the same. I hope you find a new match soon."

Miss Mae's face broke into a sunny smile. "I believe I have." She picked up Andi's hands and squeezed. "I saw your palomino this morning and described her to Mr. Coleman. He agrees she would be the perfect match for Corona."

What? Andi tore her hands from Miss Mae's grip and backed up. A lump clogged her throat. She couldn't speak. She couldn't breathe. Taffy join the circus? No! Andi shook her head.

"Don't be in such a hurry to say no," Miss Mae said. "Mr. Coleman is willing to pay *five hundred dollars* for the right palomino."

Henry gasped. "That's a heap of money, Andi."

Andi shook her head and backed up another step. Five hundred dollars or five *thousand* dollars didn't matter. She would never sell Taffy.

Miss Mae's smiley face turned dark. She no longer looked pretty. She folded her arms across her shimmery cape and tapped her foot. "Now listen here, young lady. We'll ask your folks. They could probably use five hundred—"

"No, ma'am." Melinda stepped up beside Andi. "Our family doesn't need five hundred dollars. We own the biggest ranch in the valley." She swallowed and took Andi's hand. "Even if we were dirt poor, we'd never sell my sister's horse."

The lump in Andi's throat melted. *Thank You, God, for giving me a brave sister!*

Miss Mae let out a long, slow breath like a leaky balloon. "Mr. Coleman will see about that." She glared at Melinda.

Andi tugged on her sister's hand. "Let's go."

"Thank you, Henry, for showing us around," Melinda said politely. "It's been an honor to look behind the scenes and meet the performers. But it's nearly six o'clock. Andi and I need to go."

Without waiting for Cory, the girls turned around and walked away from the circus grounds.

⊰ ⊱

Andi did not enjoy her supper at the hotel. Every time she thought about the show, Miss Minnie Mae came to mind. A hollow feeling crept into Andi's heart. Her daydream of riding Taffy through a ring of fire and dazzling the crowds fizzled.

Miss Mae wants to buy Taffy. Andi shivered, even though the hotel dining room was roasting in the August heat.

Andi took a tiny bite of chicken and let Melinda do all the talking.

Melinda's chicken and mashed potatoes and gravy turned cold. She gushed over Stewart Robinson, the handsome young trapeze artist.

"He held me up and helped me walk across a real tightrope." Her blue eyes sparkled. "All of the

Robinsons can do it, even the littlest girl, who must be only five or six."

Melinda chattered on and on. Her supper grew colder. When she got to the part about the matched pair of bareback horses, Andi pricked up her ears. What would Mother say about the circus's offer to buy Taffy?

Mother didn't say anything, but Chad had plenty to say. Like always.

"What kind of nonsense is that?" He looked at Andi. "You should have told Miss Mae that her boss is welcome to ride out to the ranch any time he likes and look over our stock. I'm sure we could find him another palomino."

He grinned. "And for a whole lot less than five hundred dollars."

"I don't think they're looking for a green broke horse," Melinda said. "They haven't time to train him from scratch. They also want one that looks just like Corona."

Chad took a swallow of water. "Well then, that's too bad for them."

By the time peach pie arrived, Andi had cheered up enough to talk about Henry. She shared how sorry he was for running away to join the circus, and how much he wanted to go home.

"Henry's all alone," Andi said. "He'll never earn enough money to go home. Even if he does, mean ol' Truckee won't let him go. Henry doesn't think his aunt and uncle love him. Worse, they don't even know where he is."

"Poor little boy," Mother said.

Andi scraped the last bite of peach pie from her plate. "Can't you do something, Justin? You're a lawyer. Lawyers are supposed to help people, right?"

Justin nodded thoughtfully. "I'll look into it as soon as I get a chance, but I can't do anything about it tonight." He drew a napkin across his face. "It's getting late. We should head home."

Chad and Mitch stayed in town to visit with friends, but Justin drove Mother, Melinda, and a sleepy Andi out to the ranch. The sun had set long before they pulled in. The stars twinkled brightly in the dark sky.

Yawning, Andi climbed out of the surrey. She grabbed one of the surrey's lanterns and stumbled toward the barn.

"Make it a quick good-night, Andrea," Mother called. "It's late."

When Andi whistled, Taffy trotted inside from her paddock behind the barn. She raised her head over the stall railing and nibbled Andi's hair.

Andi dropped an armful of alfalfa into Taffy's hayrack. Then she hugged her filly.

"Good night, Taffy. I love you."

ᵈ CHAPTER 10 ᵇ

Andi's Great Idea

Andi slept late the next morning. She didn't wake up until Melinda shook her.

"Go away." Andi pulled the covers over her head and rolled over. "I'm tired." The circus performance had worn her out, just like Mother had said it would.

Melinda shook her harder. "Get up, sleepyhead. We're going to be late for Sunday school."

"Uh-uh."

"Better hurry before Chad dumps cold water on you."

At Melinda's warning, Andi tore off her bedcovers and sprang out of bed. Last fall, she'd refused to get up on the first day of school. Big mistake. The splash of cold water on her face had cured Andi from ever again staying in bed longer than she should.

She rubbed her eyes and glanced around her room. Was big brother lurking at the door with a cup of water?

No sign of Chad. Andi relaxed.

Giggling at the success of her plan, Melinda plopped down on the bed.

Andi gave her sister a shove then quickly dressed. She pulled on her hot, scratchy stockings and buttoned her high-top shoes.

"Hurry, girls!" Mother called from the bottom of the stairs. "Your breakfast is getting cold."

Andi had no time to do more than brush out her hair. Melinda tied it back with a ribbon. Together they raced down the stairs.

Andi headed for the kitchen door, but Mother called her back. "You fed Taffy late last night. She'll keep until after church. Or she can find a bit of grass in her paddock. Come and sit down."

"Yes'm." Andi found her seat . . . and quickly made a face.

Oatmeal was not her favorite breakfast. Cold oatmeal had to be the worst breakfast in the world. She didn't say a word, though. Instead, she dumped half a pitcher of cream on the soggy cereal and forced herself to eat it.

After three bites, Andi looked up. She and Melinda were the only family members left at the table.

Uh-oh. Andi ate faster.

By the time Andi climbed into the surrey, the oatmeal had settled into a queasy lump in her stomach. The long ride into town didn't help. But she perked up when Justin drove past the circus grounds on the way to church.

The field buzzed in a beehive of activity. Tents were collapsing. People scurried about, tearing down equipment and rolling up canvases. Elephants trumpeted. Wagon wheels creaked. Above all the racket, men shouted orders.

Clearly, the circus did not take a rest on Sunday.

Andi spun around and watched the circus pack up. "It's kind of sad," she said when the surrey turned a corner and blocked her view. She returned to her seat.

"What's sad?" Melinda asked.

Andi sighed. "Seeing the circus pack up and leave isn't nearly as fun as watching it set up. It went by so fast."

Mother smiled at Andi. "A circus can't afford to stay longer than one day in a town as small as Fresno," she explained. "That's why it's called a traveling circus."

"It's sure a lot of work," Melinda said. "Do you know where they're headed next?"

"I believe they're bound for San Francisco," Mother replied. "However, they'll probably stop at one or two towns along the way."

Hang posters to announce the coming circus. Unload the wagons from the train. Organize a street parade. Set up circus tents. Practice their acts. Perform two shows. Take down the tents. Pack up. Load the wagons back on the flatbed cars. Go to the next town. Over and over, all season long.

No wonder Henry wanted to go home.

All during Sunday school and church, Andi thought about Henry. When she closed her eyes to pray, she saw his thin, dirty face and the heavy snack tray. When Reverend Harris talked on and on, Henry's sobs echoed in Andi's head.

Truckee was mean to Henry. He knocked him around and cheated him. Henry was too young and too scrawny to do anything about it. He couldn't run away. He had no money. Even if he had all the money in the world, the candy seller would just haul him back.

Unless . . .

Andi's eyes flew open during the closing prayer. *Unless Henry had a place to hide.*

Her heart beat faster than a galloping horse. It was so simple! Henry could stay on the ranch. Truckee would never find him there.

As soon as Reverend Harris said "amen," Andi looked to Mother to share her great idea.

Too late. Mrs. Evans had cornered Mother for what looked like a long, one-sided conversation.

Mother would be busy for at least another twenty minutes.

Andi ran out of the church. She had to find Henry before the circus left town.

Three blocks away, circus wagons were lining up near the railroad depot. Heaps of equipment lay piled around the wagons. From the look of things, it would take all afternoon to load up.

Andi's heart slowed down. There was still time. *Please help me find Henry*, she prayed, looking around.

Across the street, Henry stood next to the Fresno Hotel. He was wetting down the circus posters and peeling them off the wall.

Andi grinned. This was her quickest answer to prayer ever!

"Henry!" She crossed the street waving. "I'm so glad I found you. I have a great idea. Come back to the ranch with me. My brother Justin is a lawyer. He can help you get home. I know he can. And nobody will ever find—"

"No!" Henry snapped.

Andi drew back, startled. "What's wrong?"

Henry jumped down from the crate he was standing on. He yanked at the poster's lower corner. His hands shook. "Nothing's wrong. I just don't wanna leave the circus." He ripped away the paper and crumpled it. "Can't talk right now. I got work to do."

85

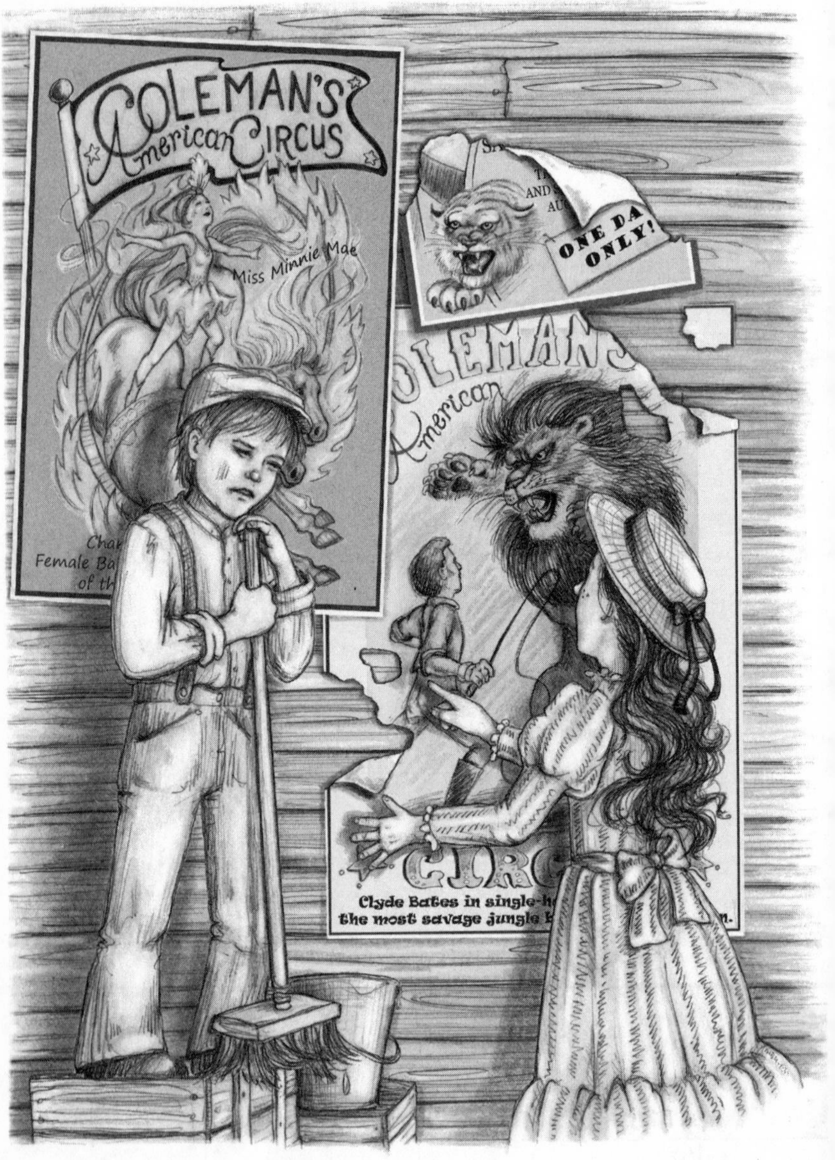
COLEMAN'S
American CIRCUS
Miss Minnie Mae
ONE DA
ONLY!
OLEMANS
American
Clyde Bates in single-h
the most savage jungle b

Andi's stomach turned over. Something was terribly wrong. Henry's face looked whiter than the poster paste he was scraping from the building. Dark circles rimmed his eyes. His shoulders were slumped.

Worse, he looked scared.

"Leave me alone." Henry turned his back on Andi and started in on the next poster.

Andi heard a muffled sob. "Henry?"

"Go away!"

Stunned, Andi turned and fled. She dashed across the street. Sweat poured down her face, but she didn't stop. Henry needed help.

It took Andi ten minutes to find Justin. When she did, she shifted impatiently from one foot to the other, waiting for a chance to talk. Children did not interrupt a lawyer and a judge, not even if the lawyer was one's oldest and favorite brother.

Judge Wallace finally shook Justin's hand and moved away.

"What's the trouble?" Justin shoved back his hat and grinned down at Andi. "You look wound up tighter than a top."

"It's Henry. Something's wrong. Can you help him? Please?"

Justin nodded. "I'll try. Where is he?"

"Across the street." Andi yanked on Justin's hand. "He's tearing down the circus posters. Hurry."

Andi pulled Justin out of the church, down the

steps, and across the yard. She pointed. "He's over . . ." Her words trailed off.

The Fresno Hotel's wall was empty of posters. The crate was gone.

And Henry was nowhere in sight.

CHAPTER 11

Henry's Secret

Justin listened to Andi's tale about Henry. When she finished, he shook his head. "I'm sorry, honey. It sounds like the boy prefers to stay with the circus."

"He doesn't," Andi insisted. "Not really. Can't we look for him?"

"And do what when we find him?" Justin asked patiently. "We can't force him to leave. It's sad, but we have to let him go."

Andi slumped. Why had Henry changed his mind? What had frightened him into staying with the circus?

Justin held out his hand. "Let's go home."

One cheerful thought stayed with Andi during the drive home: she could ride Taffy up to her special spot this afternoon and not think so much about Henry. Andi stayed in good spirits while she changed out of her Sunday clothes. She smiled through Sunday dinner.

I'm coming, Taffy!

Andi ate as fast as she could without Mother or Melinda scolding her for unladylike manners. She cleared her dishes, slammed through the back door, and jumped off the porch.

"Taffy!" She listened for her filly's answering whinny.

Silence.

She skipped into the barn and whistled.

There was no answer. No loud nickers. No impatient snorts.

Andi climbed over the stall railing and ran out to the paddock behind the barn. "Taffy!"

The paddock was empty.

A huge fist squeezed Andi's heart. "Taffy!" she screamed. Then she ran.

By the time she burst into the house, Andi was sobbing uncontrollably. "Taffy's gone!"

The rest of the family was relaxing in the large sitting room. They shot up from their seats. Mother's book thudded to the floor.

She drew Andi into her arms. "Calm down, sweetheart. Are you sure she's gone?"

Andi nodded. She untangled herself from Mother and threw herself at Chad. "Where can she be?" Tears streamed down her face. "You have to find her, Chad. You *have* to!"

"Take it easy." Chad wrapped Andi in a tight hug. "Taffy can't be far. She probably jumped the fence."

Andi gulped back her sobs. Miss Mae's determined look came to mind. "D-did the circus steal her?"

"Don't be silly. How could anybody do that without us knowing?" Chad smoothed back Andi's dark curls and kissed her forehead. "Don't worry, little sister. We'll find her."

Andi smiled through her tears. "Promise?"

"You bet. Even if we have to search every hill and valley on this ranch."

Justin, Chad, and Mitch spent the rest of the day looking for Taffy. A dozen ranch hands helped them. They searched all afternoon and late into the evening.

Andi sat on the back porch with her head propped up in her hands. She watched and waited, sniffing back her tears. And she prayed. *Please, God, show Chad where Taffy is.*

The sun went down. Darkness settled over the ranch, but her brothers did not return.

Mother joined Andi. "It's late, sweetheart. Come to bed."

Andi shook her head. "Why doesn't God answer?"

Mother took Andi's hand and gently led her back inside the house and up to change for bed. "Be patient and trust Him. God knows how much you love Taffy." She tucked the covers around Andi and sat beside her. "I'll stay right here if you like."

Andi nodded. She held Mother's hand until she fell asleep.

⚞ ⚟

"Wake up, Andi."

Andi's eyes flew open. Her heart skipped with hope. She searched her brother's face. "Did you find her, Chad?"

"Not yet, but we found a clue."

Andi turned her face away. A huge lump caught in her throat. God had not answered her prayer.

"Be patient and trust Him."

Mother's words whispered in Andi's head. She swallowed the lump and sat up to hear more. "What clue?"

"Come downstairs and you'll see," Chad said. "Sid found him a few minutes ago, crumpled in a heap by the barn and sound asleep."

Andi wrinkled her forehead. "Found who?"

"Henry." Chad rose from Andi's bed. "The boy is exhausted. He's blubbering about palominos and the circus. Mother is trying to settle him."

"Henry?" Andi leaped out of bed. Barefoot and in her nightgown, she ran down the stairs. "Mother!"

"In here, Andrea."

Andi burst into the dining room. When she saw Henry, she stopped short.

The little boy sat at the table—rumpled, dirty, and white-faced. His shaking hands held a cup of steaming chocolate, but he looked too scared to drink it.

"Go on, Henry," Mother was saying. "Take a sip. You'll feel better."

Henry obeyed. His round blue eyes met Andi's over the rim of his cup. He swallowed three big gulps and put the chocolate down. "I'm s-sorry, Andi. I did it. I wish I hadn't. But I did."

"You see?" Chad came around and took a seat next to Mother. "He's babbling."

Andi sat down across from Henry. They looked at each other for a full minute. Henry's eyes were full of apology. What had he done?

All of a sudden, an icy chill raced up Andi's spine. "You took Taffy."

Henry's eyes filled with tears. He nodded and buried his head in his arms. Huge, wracking sobs shook his shoulders.

"How did you manage that?" Chad asked.

Henry raised his head and wiped his eyes. "I saw your wagon in town Saturday after the evening show. It was dark, so I climbed under the canvas and waited."

Chad's eyebrows went up. "I see."

"When you and your brother got back to the ranch, I slipped out and hid around back. Later, I found the palomino. I put a bridle on her and rode her into town." He shrugged. "It was easy."

Andi sat tongue-tied while Henry's story unfolded.

His watery eyes pleaded for understanding. "They made me do it, Andi. I didn't want to, but Mr. Coleman found some money in my bedroll. Said I stole it." He trembled. "I never did. But Truckee said I'd go to jail unless—"

"Unless you did exactly as they told you," Mother finished.

Henry nodded. "I knew I'd done a bad thing, specially when I saw Andi yesterday. She wanted to help me." He began crying again. "So when the circus train left town last night, I snuck away. I walked all night to come back and tell Andi I was sorry."

Chad whistled. "That's a twelve-mile walk, boy."

No wonder Henry looked so grubby and tired.

"Yes, sir," Henry said. "I decided I'd rather go to jail than stay with that circus even one more day."

Andi's head spun. Henry could be as sorry as he liked, but what about Taffy? His apology hadn't brought her filly home. She found her tongue.

"Where's Taffy now? And how do I get her back?"

⊰ CHAPTER 12 ⊱

Home Sweet Home

Andi clenched her fists and waited for Henry's answer. She had felt sorry for him and wanted to help. She'd offered to hide him on the ranch.

Fury burned in her belly. The whole time she'd been talking to him yesterday, Henry knew he'd been on the Circle C. *Henry is a sneaky horse thief.*

"Taffy is most likely with the circus, Andrea," Mother answered for Henry. "But your brothers will get her back."

"That's a promise." Chad rose from the table and brushed Mother's cheek with a kiss. "I'll grab Mitch, and we'll ask Sheriff Tate to join us. Don't know how long we'll be gone. We might not be able to catch up with the circus until they stop at the next town."

He ruffled Andi's hair on his way out.

Silence fell.

"Please don't be mad at me, Andi," Henry pleaded. "I'm sorry."

Andi sat still as a stone. She didn't want to forgive Henry. Until she wrapped her arms around Taffy's neck, it felt much better to stay angry.

"Andrea," Mother said quietly, "I hope you realize it took a lot of courage for Henry to walk out to the ranch and own up to what he did. He could have left town with the circus. If he had, we'd never have known for sure what happened to Taffy."

Mother's words pricked Andi's heart. How many times had Andi done something wrong and later wished she hadn't? Mother was right. It was hard to own up and say you're sorry.

Henry wasn't a horse thief. He was a hero.

Andi bowed her head. Her heart pounded. She knew what she had to do. "Thank you, Henry." She looked up. "I'm still scared that I might not get Taffy back, but I'm glad you tried to make it right."

The little boy's face lit up. "You're not mad?"

Andi smiled and shook her head. "Not enough to matter."

Henry laughed. He slurped the rest of his chocolate and looked around for something to eat. Soon he was munching on a piece of toast.

Melinda and Justin joined the family for breakfast

just then. Luisa brought in a platter of eggs and more toast. Henry piled his plate high.

Justin chuckled. "Looks like you're feeling better, young man."

Henry nodded, his mouth full of eggs.

"You'll feel even better when you hear that I'm going to send a telegram to your aunt and uncle this morning," Justin said.

Henry stopped chewing. His eyes grew huge.

"Do you think you can find them?" Andi asked. "And Henry can go home?"

"I plan to give it my best try, honey." Justin winked and dug into his breakfast.

⚞ ⚟

The next day a telegram arrived at the ranch. Aunt Myrtle and Uncle Hank had been very worried about Henry. They were glad to receive Justin's news and wanted their nephew home.

"They're awful poor," Henry said when Justin finished reading the telegram. "And it costs a lot of money to bring me home. I haven't got a dime except for the one you gave me during the show on Saturday."

He reached into his pants pocket and pulled out the ten-cent piece. "It's not much, but—"

"Keep it," Justin said, smiling. "Sharing your secret about Taffy is at least worth a railway ticket home."

Henry sucked in an astonished breath. "You mean it, sir?"

Justin nodded. "I do."

"Oh, Mr. Carter," Henry said in a rush. "Thank you! I sure learned my lesson. I won't ever leave my aunt and uncle again. And I'll never, ever say another sorry word about having to ride Uncle Hank's plow horse either."

Henry's smile reached from ear to ear. "They were worried about me. They really missed me."

Andi listened, her heart torn in two. Half of her cheered for the little circus boy who could finally go home. The other half of her heart hurt for Taffy. Had Chad and Mitch found her?

While Justin made arrangements to send Henry home, Andi watched and waited for a telegram from her brothers. One day went by. Then two. Then three. Still no telegram.

Andi spent the long, scary days showing Henry around the ranch. On the fourth day, she and Henry sat on the straw in Taffy's stall. Andi stared at the empty hayrack and tried not to cry. Chad had *promised* to bring her filly back. Why didn't he or Mitch send word that they had caught up with the circus?

Andi had asked that question every day, so there

was no use asking it again. Especially not to Henry. She pushed her worries aside for the hundredth time that day and said, "I can't believe you're going to ride the train for three days all by yourself."

Henry chewed on a piece of straw. "Why not? I rode the circus train all summer." He grinned. "Your mother is sending along a wicker basket of food. I'll travel like a king." He puffed out his chest.

As much as Andi hurt inside, she couldn't help getting caught up in Henry's excitement. "I've ridden the train before," she said. "We always go up to the state fair in—"

"Andi! Where are you? *Come quick!*"

Melinda's shriek sent Andi flying out of Taffy's stall, with Henry at her heels. Her heart slammed against the inside of her chest. What was wrong? Melinda never screamed.

Andi pushed past the barn's wide double doors looking for her sister.

Melinda pointed. "Look, Andi. They're back!"

Dusty, grubby, and unshaven, Chad and Mitch trotted into the yard. A third horse followed on a lead rope.

Taffy!

Dizzy with joy, Andi shrieked and dashed to the riders.

Chad dropped from his saddle and caught her up. "Told you we'd find her, didn't I?"

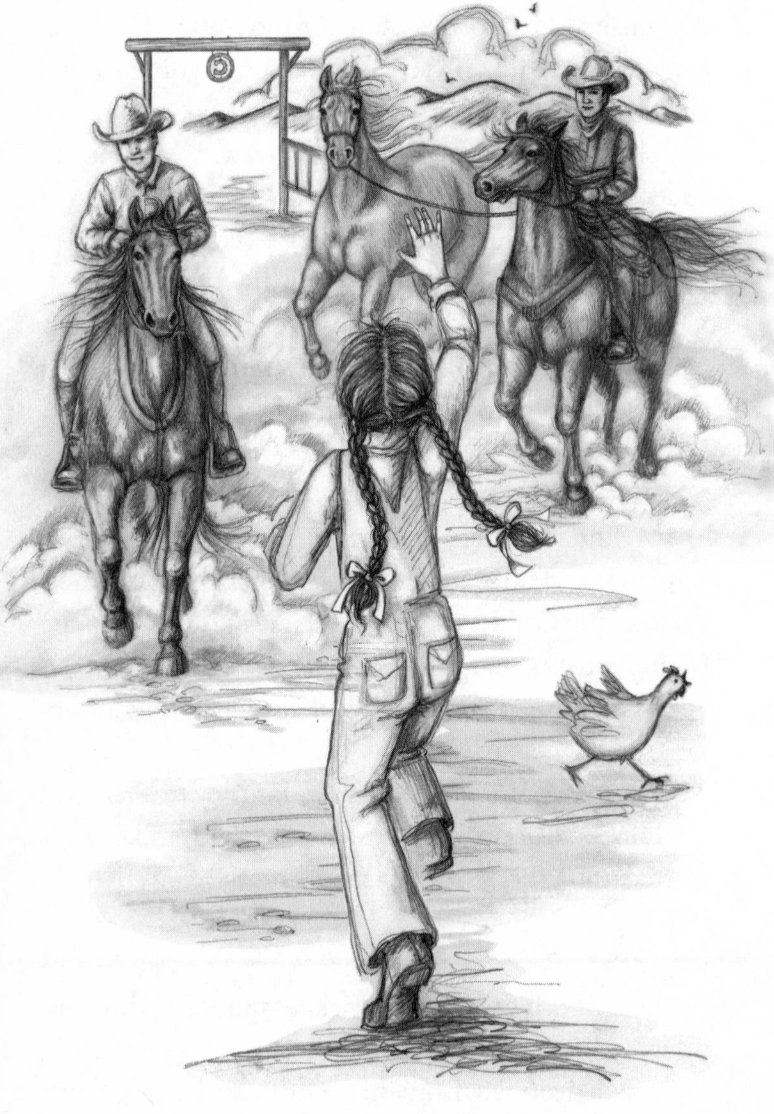

Andi squeezed him gratefully. "Yes, but you never sent a telegram. I waited and waited."

"You can't send a telegram if they're repairing the lines," Mitch said, grinning. "Besides, the look on your face was worth the surprise."

Andi gave Chad another grateful hug then wriggled out of his arms. She hugged Mitch then raced to her filly.

"Taffy!" She threw her arms around Taffy's neck. Tears stung her eyes. *Thank you, Jesus!*

A scuffling in the dust reminded Andi she had someone else to thank. She pulled herself away from Taffy's golden coat and saw Henry smiling shyly at her.

Andi smiled back. "Thank you, Henry. You helped bring Taffy home."

Henry nodded. "And now I'm going home too."

History Fun
Here Comes the Circus!

An 1800s circus was a colorful world of amazement and delight. One of the biggest events of the year, it offered an exciting break from everyday life. A week or two before the circus train rolled in, advance men plastered advertising posters all over town. The big, colorful posters were very detailed and the only way people could learn about the upcoming attractions. There was no TV or Internet that long ago.

For many people, especially in small towns, the circus was the only opportunity to see monkeys, giraffes, tigers, and other animals that are now found in zoos. It was also their only chance to watch acrobats, bicyclists, jugglers, and trapeze artists perform. Bareback trick riders were especially popular.

The first circus opened in 1768 in England and was limited to horsemanship acts. Eventually, other performances were added—even full acted-out battles and chariot races! These circuses were housed in large buildings that stayed in one place. The circus first came to the United States in 1793. George Washington, our first president, attended this American circus in Philadelphia, Pennsylvania.

During Andi's day (in the mid 1800s), big-top circuses became popular. Canvas tents made it easy to move the circus from town to town. With railroads booming, circuses traveled all over the country, bringing the excitement of circus life to thousands of people.

Kids, especially boys, were often tempted to run away and join the circus. Dreary day-to-day farm chores couldn't compare to the apparent freedom and thrills of the big top—exotic animals, cheering crowds, a chance to see the country. Sadly, many children in the 1800s were not treated well, especially orphans.

There have been over a hundred different circuses through the years. Most are named after their owners. In 1919, two circuses merged. The Barnum & Bailey Greatest Show on Earth joined with the

Ringling Bros. World's Greatest Show to become the Ringling Bros. and Barnum & Bailey Combined Shows. This most well-known of all American circuses is still active today, presenting The Greatest Show on Earth throughout the United States.

**For more Andi fun,
download free activity pages
at CircleCSteppingStones.com.**

Susan K. Marlow is always on the lookout for a new story, whether she's writing books, teaching writing workshops, or sharing what she's learned as a homeschooling mom. Susan is the author of several series set in the Old West—ranging from new reader to young adult—and she enjoys relaxing on her fourteen-acre homestead in the great state of Washington. Connect with the author at CircleCSteppingStones.com or by emailing Susan at SusanKMarlow@kregel.com.

Leslie Gammelgaard, illustrator of the Circle C Beginnings and Circle C Stepping Stones series, lives in beautiful Washington state where every season delights the senses. Along with illustrating books, Leslie inspires little people (especially her four grandchildren) to explore and express their creative nature through art and writing.

Grow Up with Andi!

Don't miss any of Andi's adventures in the Circle C Beginnings series

Andi's Pony Trouble
Andi's Indian Summer
Andi's Fair Surprise
Andi's Scary School Days
Andi's Lonely Little Foal
Andi's Circle C Christmas

**Visit AndiandTaffy.com
for free coloring pages,
learning activities, and more!**

For readers ages 9–13!

Andi's adventures continue in the Circle C Adventures series

Andrea Carter and the Long Ride Home
Andrea Carter and the Dangerous Decision
Andrea Carter and the Family Secret
Andrea Carter and the San Francisco Smugglers
Andrea Carter and the Trouble with Treasure
Andrea Carter and the Price of Truth

Free enrichment activities are available at
CircleCAdventures.com.